Charles Lambert is the author of several novels, short stories, and the memoir *With a Zero at its Heart*, which was voted one of *The Guardian* readers' Ten Best Books of the Year in 2014.

In 2007, he won an O. Henry Award for his short story 'The Scent of Cinnamon'. His first novel, *Little Monsters*, was longlisted for the 2010 International IMPAC Dublin Literary Award. Born in England, Charles Lambert has lived in central Italy since 1980.

Two Dark Tales:

Jack Squat

and

The Niche

Charles Lambert

AARDVARK
BUREAU

Two Dark Tales:

Jack Squat
and
The Niche

Charles Lambert

Aardvark Bureau
London
An imprint of Gallic Books

An Aardvark Bureau Book
An imprint of Gallic Books

First published in Great Britain in 2017 by
Aardvark Bureau, 59 Ebury Street, London, SW1W 0NZ

A CIP record for this book is available from the British Library
ISBN 978-1-910709-29-0

Typeset in Garamond Pro by Aardvark Bureau
Printed in the UK by CPI
(CR0 4YY)

2 4 6 8 10 9 7 5 3 1

The Niche

1

Billy Lender is crouched between the pushed-out cupboard and the wall, as deep into the niche as he can get. His shorts are tickling the back of his knee, but he can't move to scratch himself because he might be heard. Behind his head, the radiator gurgles, loud in his ear, scalding hot. If it touches his hand, or the back of his neck, where his hair has just been cut, he'll get burnt, and give the game away. All he can hear above the gurgle is Mad Millie shouting in the room at the far end of the corridor, in history class, where Billy ought to be this minute. He'd better move now, or he'll be in even worse trouble. But how can he trust the silence to mean he's safe? He doesn't dare think what Mad Millie will do to him for being late. He slapped Jenkins round the head so hard once, for whispering in class, they both lost their balance and Jenkins had blood come out of his ear. He's going to have to risk it.

Billy edges a half-dead foot out from beneath his leg. The cupboard shifts. He stops, holding his breath, waits for the pins and needles to ease up. If only he'd made it to the library in time, he'd have been safe. He'd have walked out with the others and been at his desk, with Mad Millie writing dates on the board and everyone copying them down in their rough books, ready for homework.

When he nerves himself to straighten his leg, he hears a low voice. 'Gobface.' He freezes. The voice is a baby voice, the way they say he sounds. He can't tell who it is. Horton, Sharples, one of the Lees twins. The worst is Sharples. 'Gobface.' A giggle, something banging against the wall. 'We know where you are.' The voice dragged out as long as the words will go, still in the voice they say is his, Baby Billy, Baby Gobface Billy, like a worm in the ear. 'Come on, Gobface.'

The weight of his whole body on the bent ankle is too much to bear as the feeling rushes back. His eyes fill with tears. When he hears it a third time – not one voice now, but voices, a chorus of voices; Gobface, says the chorus, and giggles, and a second thump, closer now – he stifles a sob. His other leg is dead. His throat is dry. Pressed back into the wall, into the niche in the wall, he feels the scorch of the radiator on the back of his head. After a second, two seconds, five, he can smell something singe. He jerks his head away. The cupboard beside him rattles.

'He's here.' The voice only feet away now. 'I can smell him. What a stink. I bet he's shit himself.' They laugh. He shrinks down into his bones and skin, as small as he can get; he's scared they can hear his heart. Does he stink? Has he shit himself? Cautious, he sniffs the air. Sweat in his eyes makes them smart.

This is when he feels it, like a breath on his cheek, or a breeze from below, an earthy smell. He flinches, raises his hand to touch where the breath has been, as though to capture it, hold it against him. But he forgets about the breath immediately when the footsteps stop and he sees fingers curl round the side of the cupboard to shift it from the wall. He braces his back against the radiator. He'll fight if he has to, he decides. He will.

'What do you wretched boys think you're doing?'

The fingers disappear. He feels the breath again, come back like something cool, a damp cloth to calm fever, almost a whisper.

'Is that Sharples I can see, crouching in gnome-like fashion behind his accomplices?'

'Yes, sir.'

'Come here, you hopeless child.'

He hears footsteps, a slap, a muffled cry. The nearest feet shuffle. Their turn next, he thinks, gleeful. Their turn to suffer.

'Now get into whichever class you're supposed to be in, all four of you, and God help whomever of my esteemed colleagues is expected to teach you anything.'

More footsteps, moving away from him this time, then safety swilling in to fill the space, like water, the parquet shining with it. Messerschmitt to the rescue, thinks Billy.

'And if I see any one of your loutish faces skulking around the corridors again, under any circumstances, any circumstances whatsoever, it will be my pleasure to introduce you once again to my old friend George. I think you've already been acquainted with George, Sharples. Am I right? Your rotund young backside and George are old friends. And that applies to Lees One and Two. Yes, that's correct, you two. Only Horton remains to be introduced. Am I right? Because that can soon be arranged.'

'Yes, sir.' One voice. Sharples? It sounds like Sharples.

'I'm sorry?'

'Yes, sir.' Chorus of voices.

'That's better. No one likes boys that mumble. Now be off with you, you miserable rabble, before I lose my temper.'

Billy doesn't think about the breath until he's in bed, almost asleep. He hears it again, but inside his ear this time, as though something has lodged there and is slowly moving, settling itself in. He tries to hold his own breath to hear it better, but just as suddenly as it started, the noise is gone. He lies still for what feels like hours, unable to sleep, until the house is silent around him, then reaches beneath the pillow and pulls out his torch and the magazine he stole from the shop when he went in for sweets. There's a man on the cover, his shirt ripped off, tied down by ropes to rocks, with crabs crawling over the rocks towards him. The name of the magazine is *Rugged Men*. He misread it the first time: he thought it said *Rugger Men* – he had to look in the dictionary to find out what 'rugged' meant. The caption, in bright-red letters with spiked yellow edges like lightning, says the man is being subjected to a torture invented by the Japanese army for prisoners of war. His face is twisted with pain as he strains against the ropes. A crab is crawling across his thigh towards the scrap of cloth that covers the private parts between his legs. Another crab is biting into the ball of his thumb with scissor-edged pincers. Billy feels something stir between his own bare legs, something he doesn't understand, an unexpected clenching of his flesh against the prospect of pain.

Sharples is the worst. He's the biggest of the four. Big and heavy at the shoulders, with big fat legs, and trousers too tight for them. He has long hair down over his forehead, flopping into his eyes, and patches of red on each cheek. His hands are big, with dull red swollen knuckles as though he's just hit a wall with them. Billy saw him do this once, over and over until they bled, his gang of friends clapping in time to egg him on, to cover the grunting noise he made each time he did it. There was plaster on the floor, like crusted snow. He wiped the blood off on Horton's shirt. Horton told him to bugger off and Sharples punched him so hard in the stomach Horton crumpled to the floor. He rolled around for ages, holding his stomach, sucking in air. When he stood up, Sharples laughed. Everyone laughed. Horton had snot all over his chin. I'll fucking kill you, he said. They were friends again by the time the bus came.

Horton is small and thin, with a pinched nose and lips, and curly blond hair cut shorter at the back and sides than other people. He looks like a poodle, Billy thinks but doesn't dare say. Horton likes to walk around the classroom as if he owns it until Sharples tells him to sit down or a master comes in. Mad Millie grabbed him by his curls once when he was caught talking and banged his head on the desk. Horton just sat there afterwards, pulling loose hair from his head until he had a little pile of golden curls on the desk. Billy thought and hoped Mad Millie would hit him again but he didn't. At the end of the lesson he told Horton to stop playing the fool and to throw the hair into the bin. 'Oh,' said Horton, 'but I wanted to give it to my mother, to stuff a pin cushion.' 'That's enough insolence from you,' said Mad Millie. After that, some boys called Horton *Pin Cushion* until Sharples bollocked one of them. Billy was careful not to laugh. The Lees twins already had their eyes on him, and their mouths ready to tell tales, and their hands ready to hold him down. They were the ones who picked him out from the others. Billy had thought they might be friends at first, after they'd all been introduced to George, but he was wrong about that.

That was months ago now, when they were all new boys. They came before him in the alphabet. It was Messerschmitt's fault, and George's.

First day. Trooping from room to room. They copied their timetables into their new beige exercise books, and taped in a map of the school on shiny paper, all before morning break. Billy was scared of every corner, every face and door, looking for somewhere safe to hide himself. But the world was in motion, no place stayed put. Each teacher had his own name, Reynolds (harelip), Wilkinson (tall, bent, big nose), Martin (short, shiny black hair, moustache). Billy tried to remember them all, but already the other boys were coming up with other names. Foxy. Konk. Mad Millie. Some made sense to Billy, some not. He stared at the twins until they noticed him, then hurriedly looked away.

The first lesson they spent in their own room, the last in a row of rooms built out of wood, windows at each side, sticking out from the old redbrick body of the school. Their form master's name was Mr Wolf, and that was what they called him, but without the Mr – Wolf was enough. He had a bald head, smooth and white as a peeled egg, and bright blue eyes. He was all smiles, sitting on the edge of his desk, one hand holding an ankle while he told them what they would do with him. English and cricket. He called them his little men.

Billy had started to relax, when a boy behind him interrupted. Wolf bared his teeth, and growled. He had canines that caught on his bottom lip. 'Stand up, boy,' he said. The boy stood up, giggling nervously. No one knew if Wolf was putting on an act. 'Come here,' he said, wiggling his finger. 'That's my little man.'

The boy walked past Billy's desk. Billy saw his bare knees shake. They were all wearing thick brown shorts, like felt; they would wear them until the Christmas holidays had finished. Easter term, the taller ones would move on to long trousers. Billy didn't expect to be tall enough for that, although he dreamt he might be. One of the boy's socks had slipped down, the brown and orange stripes round his ankle like a ruff. Billy checked his own as the boy stood in front of Wolf, waiting. The boy was Horton, but Billy didn't know that until Wolf asked him. Wolf told Horton to pass him the board rubber. When he had it in his hand, with Horton standing in front of him, Wolf passed the rubber from hand to hand, as if he was weighing it, back and forth, back and forth, his eyes on Horton's eyes, until, when Horton was looking down at his feet, the blood gone from his face, Wolf slipped the soft part of the board rubber under his chin to lift his head.

'Put this back where it was,' he said. Horton took it from his hand and put it back. He had blue chalk on his chin, like a beard. Walking past Billy's desk, he saw Billy see the chalk, and smile.

'I'll get you,' he said, under his breath. 'I'll get you outside.'

But he didn't. Billy sneaked out behind the backs of other boys and into the old school. No one saw him. He didn't know where he could go and where he couldn't; he didn't have the map they'd given him after assembly.

He came to an open door that led onto the drive at the front of the school. Sunlight was pouring into the dark place where Billy stood. He stepped back as a bunch of older boys, men almost, jostled in through the door, legs caked with flecks of dried mud, rugby shorts, boots, shouting, pushing against one another, the smell of them, sweat and something stinging, medicinal, new to him.

The last boy to come through the door was detached by a matter of seconds from the rest of the bunch. He was silent, different from the others, bigger and brighter. When some voice called from the drive behind, he paused, only inches from Billy, to answer. The sunlight on his legs was gold, the fine hairs one shade lighter than the gold of the skin, gold woven and spun, silkier than thread. Back pressed against the wall, Billy lost his breath. When he found it the boy was gone and there was a bell ringing to remind him of the world. He would have to run hard to get back to where he'd been, where he was supposed to be, along a corridor where running was forbidden. He thought he might never get there, never again be where he had been only moments before.

General Science began with the compilation of the register. They were told to sit on high stools behind long wooden desks with deep white sinks and gas taps for Bunsen burners. Messerschmitt (bull-necked, glasses) told them to stand up one by one and call out their names in alphabetical order. Billy waited. Someone called Lawson stood up, said, 'Lawson,' sat down. Billy stood up, said, 'Lender.'

When the register was finished, Messerschmitt counted the names. 'Two short,' he said. He looked through his glasses, great square face screwed into a scowl. He had big hands; he rubbed them together, like someone who needed warming up. Nobody moved until one of the twins put up his hand.

'Lees, sir. My name's Lees.'

Messerschmitt nodded. 'Stand up, boy.' He turned his head to nod a second time. 'You too, boy.'

The twins were three rows in front of Billy. They stood up together. There was a space between them as they moved away from each other. Messerschmitt looked down at his register, then sighed. 'You've made my register untidy,' he said. 'That won't do at all.' He beckoned them with a curling finger. 'I think it's time you two met George.' He looked at the register a second time, whistling quietly. 'And who, I wonder, was the over-precipitate boy who jumped into the breach?' He looked up. 'Which one of you sorry lot is Lender?'

George was a piece of polished wood. Two inches by two inches by eighteen, Billy found out later. First one Lees bent over, and then the other, hands on the edge of Messerschmitt's desk while Messer lifted their blazer, then stepped back.

Neither of them cried until the third and final blow. And then it was Billy's turn. When it was over, the three of them had to say, together, 'Thank you, George.'

The other boys treated the Lees twins and Billy like heroes after that. For a while, at least.

Lees and Lees were sat at his table for school dinner that first day, after they'd been introduced to George. The dining hall had seven long tables, one for each form, with thirty boys on each, and a teacher at the head, to dish out the food. Billy looked along the line of teachers. They were all there, standing behind their chairs, the ones he'd seen that morning. Messerschmitt and Wolf and the history master, Mad Millie, and Konk, tall and bent over with a bony nose, who promised he'd not speak French to them until after the Christmas holidays, and then laughed.

The only table without a teacher was his table, the first-form table, the new boys. They had a bony woman in a blue dress, with a white apron over it, and a nurse's hat pinned on her head with Kirby grips. When one of the big boys said grace, Billy opened his eyes a fraction and saw her staring along the line of boys as if she was fixing them in her head to punish them later. He closed them quickly before her eyes reached his. She told them she was Matron and she'd brook no nonsense. The food she served was a sludge of mincemeat with triangles of fried bread that splintered when Billy tried to cut his piece. His mother never cooked mincemeat; she said it was full of scraps that no one would buy if they knew what went into it. Billy felt sick. He'd have stopped eating, pushed the plate away, but Matron had started to walk round the table, behind their backs. If any boy put down his knife and fork she grabbed him by the shoulders and twisted them back until he moaned. 'Don't slouch, boy,' she said, and stood behind him until he started eating again. One boy shook salt on the food. Seconds later, she had his shoulders in her grip.

'What's your name, boy?'

'Evans, Matron.'

'Were you brought up in a fish and chip shop, Evans?'

'No, Matron,' said Evans, wincing with pain. He was opposite Billy. Billy could see both their faces: Evans almost in tears, cheeks red with shame; Matron's white lips drawn back from her teeth, eyes bright and dark, like holes.

'Well-brought-up boys put salt on the side of their plate,' she said, and gave a final twist. 'They don't sprinkle it over the whole plate like confetti at a wedding.'

Evans yelped. 'Yes, Matron,' he said, his voice breaking. Billy looked away from them, ashamed for Evans, and along the row to where the Lees twins were stifling giggles. The one on the left pulled a face at him, then grinned.

Outside the dining hall, they came across to him. 'Does your bum hurt?' they asked him. He nodded.

'Matron's not a proper woman,' Lees One said. 'Our brother told us.'

Billy nodded again.

'She's had her hole stitched up,' Lees Two said.

'Her cunt,' Lees One said.

Billy must have looked puzzled because they nudged each other, then started to laugh. 'Our brother's in the fourth form,' Lees Two said. Lees Two was taller than Lees One, by an inch at least. You could only tell them apart when they were standing side by side, Billy saw, and thought it was odd that, together, they were separate. Separate, they were one and the same.

'He tells us stuff,' said Lees One. 'That's how we know what to call them.' He nodded towards a huddle of teachers smoking outside the dining-hall door. Billy was thinking about stitched-up hole and cunt and what it meant. 'That Messerschmitt's a Kraut,' said Lees One. 'He's a Nazi, our brother says, but he got away in time. He should be in jail for being a traitor.'

Together, they took Billy into the toilets and pulled down their shorts and underpants to show him the red stripes on their arses, three stripes each, bright on the bare white skin. 'Now let's see yours,' they said, tucking their shirts back in, turning on him, but Billy shook his head. Lees Two glanced across to the door. 'No,' he said, 'not now.'

Billy breathed out. I'm safe, he thought. He wondered for how long.

The Lees twins left him alone for the rest of the day, and the day after that. Billy began to relax until, one morning the week after, they came across to him at break.

'Have you got any money?'

He shook his head.

'Don't be daft,' said Lees One, stepping up close to him. Lees Two moved round to his side, between him and the rest of the playground. Both of them were bigger than he was. He started to feel his heart beat, his palms grow damp. 'We know you have,' said Lees One. He pushed Billy's chest with both hands. 'I saw your dad give you some when he dropped you off.' He grabbed Billy's tie and slid his hand up it, tightening the knot. 'Only it isn't yours, see.'

'Leave me alone,' croaked Billy.

'"Leave me alone,"' said Lees Two in a squeaky voice. Lees One reached down with his free hand and grabbed at Billy's crotch. Billy jerked back, the tie throttling him.

'Look,' said Lees Two. 'He's dancing.' He kicked Billy's ankle. 'Go on, dance,' he said, as Billy buckled to the left. 'That's it,' he said. 'Dance for us.'

Other boys began to gather around them, eager for what promised to be a fight, until a wall had formed between Billy and the school. He moved his feet in what might have been a dance. Lees Two kicked him a second time, behind the knee, then grabbed Billy's elbow and yanked his arm down. With his leg bent after the kick, he was half kneeling, half hanging from Lees Two's grip. 'No,' he said, then, 'please.' Before he could regain his balance he was on the floor, his cheek against the concrete. I'll get my blazer dirty, he thought, as they pushed him onto his back. Lees One – or was it Two? He couldn't be sure – straddled him, heavy on his chest, his knees pinning down Billy's arms. Everything hurt. His arms, his legs where he'd been kicked, the side of his face where grit had cut into the skin. He stared up through a blur of tears to see the boy grinning, to see his mouth open, the tongue slide out, a heavy ball of spit roll from the tip of it, hang there, slowly fall. He heard a hoot of laughter before the spit hit his face. The laughter was worse than the spit, warm, so close to his mouth he could reach it with his own tongue, taste it. 'Gobface,' someone said. 'Gobface,' they all said, together. He closed his eyes.

Things got worse a few weeks later, the first afternoon they had cross-country. The entire school was lined up beside the rugby pitch, the new boys at the front; behind them, grouped by year, the rest. Billy, turning his head as they waited to be told to start, could just see the older boy from the corridor at the very back, chatting with the sports teacher. When the whistle blew, he stumbled and almost fell over as the rest of the form jostled him. Within minutes he was among the last of his group, his own form and older boys overtaking him as they streamed out of the school grounds and along a muddy lane. He had no idea how far they were supposed to be running, nor how long it would take. He was frightened he might not be strong enough to complete the course, or be left so far behind he might have no one to follow and end up lost. His running shoes, which he had never worn before that day, were too big for him; by the time five minutes had passed, before the boys had left the lane and turned into an empty field, the back of the right shoe had begun to chafe his skin. To stop it hurting, he started running in a lopsided way, wincing each time his foot hit the ground. Two of the group of stragglers around him – boys he didn't know, from the form above his – noticed this and started to laugh. He tried to run faster, to leave them all behind, gritting his teeth against the pain. By this time the rest of the school was some distance ahead, in the neighbouring field or beyond. He couldn't keep the speed up any longer and suddenly, as if a switch inside him had been flicked, he gave up trying. He was walking now, with three older boys, fat ones he'd seen hanging around together in the corner of the playground, swapping bags of sweets. They glanced across at him, unwelcoming, then broke into a ragged, breathless trot to get away from him.

He only began to jog, wincing at every step, when a distance of fifty yards had opened up. If he lost sight of everyone, he'd have no idea where to go. The route had been shown to them during the final lesson of the day, before they'd been herded into the gym to change, but he hadn't paid attention. He hated cross-country, he hated changing out of his uniform into his stiff new sports kit, he hated sport generally. He didn't see the point of being forced to run miles through muddy fields, only to end up where he'd started. He hobbled in pursuit of the fat boys, fighting back the urge to call out to them, to ask them to wait for him, knowing that it would be wasted effort. When they stopped to get their breath, bending forward with their hands on their bare red knees, he staggered past them, not pausing to look until they were some way behind. They were sharing something out among them, he couldn't see what. I won't be last back at school, he thought, and this relieved him.

He'd been out for half an hour, most of it spent walking to protect his heel, when he saw Sharples and one of the Lees twins half hidden by a hedge, their legs dangling into the ditch beneath it. As he approached, they grinned and beckoned to him to join them. Sharples held up a cigarette. Billy glanced behind to make sure no one had seen him. 'Get over here,

Gobface,' Sharples hissed. Billy walked over to them, hesitant, wishing he had seen them before they had seen him. The other Lees twin appeared from behind the hedge, tugging up his shorts. He grabbed Billy's elbow, pulling him over and pushing him down into the ditch. Sharples offered him the cigarette. When Billy shook his head, Sharples flicked ash into Billy's face. 'Whoops. Sorry,' he said, brushing it off with a slap, then held the burning tip as close to Billy's cheek as he could without touching, while the Lees twins giggled. Billy froze. Sharples stood up, his crotch at eye level. His shorts were so tight Billy could see the packet of cigarettes, a box of matches, in the pocket.

'You're coming with me, Gobface,' he said. 'I want to show you something.' Billy didn't move. He could still feel the heat from the cigarette on his face, or thought he could, as if he had really been burnt. 'I told you to come with me,' said Sharples, his voice low, menacing. 'Don't you start messing me about.' His tone changed, wheedling now. 'Come on. I won't hurt you. I just want to show you something, honest.' He pushed his hands into the front of his shorts, and for a moment Billy wondered what he meant. 'Don't I?' he said to the Lees twins, who grinned and nodded, then hauled Billy out from the ditch. His shoes were soaked, his heel was smarting where the skin had been rubbed away. He was on the point of crying.

Together, they passed through the gap in the hedge, Billy held fast between the twins, Sharples leading the way. They headed along the length of the hedge until they came to a fenced-off area, the size of a tennis court. Sharples lifted the barbed wire as high as it would go, twisted beneath it, then held it high again for the three of them to pass. The first Lees placed his hand on Billy's head, almost gently, to make sure it wasn't snagged on the wire; the second Lees ducked behind him, so close his bare leg rubbed against Billy's. When all four of them were on the other side of the fence, Sharples took Billy's arm and led him to what looked like a pile of grassed-over bricks. Billy heard the fat boys walk past beyond the hedge, talking together. He wanted to call out to them, wanted someone to know where he was, just in case, but Sharples' fingers gripped tight above his elbow and he didn't dare.

'Look at this,' said Sharples, shifting the nearest bricks to one side with his foot. Billy saw a small hole open up in the ground. The twins pulled more bricks away until the hole was the size of a well. Billy was scared of what they might do. He tried to pull away, but Sharples wrestled him to the ground in a moment. 'Oh no you don't, Gobface,' he said. 'Quick, you two, get his feet.' They pinned Billy down, his head and shoulders hanging over the hole's edge; he could see no bottom to it. He strained to lift his head away from the smell of damp earth that was filling his nostrils. When the three of them began to ease him further over the emptiness, he cried out in fear and the sound disappeared like a dropped stone into nothing. They had his arms held high behind his back; lifting them higher, they forced his head down deeper into the hole. For a moment, lifting his head up as far as it would go, he found he couldn't breathe and then he caught a whistling from far below, a high-pitched whistling that seemed to be rising towards him like a scream. He struggled to break free. Someone was sitting on his legs. 'Please let me go,' he begged. All at once the weight on his legs was gone and he was being lifted by his arms a few inches more, and then a few inches more, until the upper part of his body was entirely suspended. He was crying now. 'Please let me go,' he stuttered through his tears. He heard what sounded like an echo of his own voice, but softer, more like a whisper, and closer.

And then he was being pulled back from the edge and the other boys were running back to the fence, helping one another through the barbed wire fence, Sharples cuffing the twins round the head. He was alone. He looked at himself. He was covered in mud, his shoes were soaking wet. He wiped his face with his bare arm. Shivering, he wriggled under the barbed wire and pushed back through the hedge until he was in the lane once more. He began to half walk, half hop in the direction he thought would take him to the school.

Billy discovered the space behind the cupboard that afternoon. He was the last to arrive. When one of the prefects collared him, he used his bloodied heel as an excuse and was let off detention. The sports master sent him off to the shower, then went outside for a cigarette. Stooping to tie a shoelace, Billy found himself alone in the corridor between the playground and the changing rooms. He had just straightened up when he saw a Lees twin stick his head out through the changing-room door. He darted back against the wall, behind a store cupboard he'd never seen open, taller than he was. He heard a low hum in his ears, a sort of whispering to his right. He turned his head to see what it was.

That was when he saw the niche. There must have been something there at one time, he thought later, a hatch of some sort, a passage leading into the darkness deep below the school. Now there was only the niche, half deep enough for a boy, the radiator just overlapping one side of it, the cupboard moved away from the wall to leave space for it. He could squeeze in and not be seen, he thought. The Lees twin had gone; he hadn't been noticed. He tried the niche out for size. It was tight, but it worked. He could stay here for ever, if he needed to. The humming noise had stopped. He crouched until he was entirely hidden, picking the scabs of dried mud off his legs. The mud came off in scales, dried almost white, like clay. His leg was clean beneath it. Maybe he wouldn't need to take a shower if he waited long enough. Maybe there would be no one else there but one of the prefects, to make sure nothing happened. He thought about the prefect he'd seen that first morning, with the sunlight on him, the boy beside the sports teacher before the run that afternoon, the boy who behaved like a man. Billy knew who he was now. He was Head Boy, captain of rugger, captain of football. His name was Mitchell; he was in his final year. He took them for prep sometimes. He'd come into the class in his sports kit and sit where the teacher sat, his mud-stained boots on the desk, reading a newspaper, while Billy pretended to work, watching his bare legs shift as he turned the pages.

Someone was walking along the corridor. The sound of steps seemed louder in the silence. He didn't know who it was, and he didn't care. He wanted to laugh with relief. He'd never felt safer, not since the day he started school. He had found a place to hide in. He had found his niche.

He woke up that night and it felt as though he had been hanging there over the hole, his head pushed down into the emptiness of it, or lying there in the playground still, with the knees of the bigger boy pressing into his arms and the gravel digging into the back of his head only seconds before, as though the time between then and now had been wiped away and he would never be allowed up, allowed to stand. He was breathing hard, so hard it sounded like another person, breathing in time, beside him. He lay there in the dark, too scared to move, listening to the nameless breath.

2

After the lesson, Horton pretends to be on his side, which makes it worse. He does this sometimes. When no one else is around, if no one else is looking, he comes over to Billy and asks him what he's up to. 'We looked for you,' he says. 'We wanted to show you something. You were hiding, weren't you?' 'No,' says Billy, wary. Horton stands there, his hands in his blazer pockets, while Billy waits to see what will happen next, how deviously he might get hurt. Some mornings, at break, Horton sidles across, takes something from his pocket, a packet of gum, a tube of Smarties, and offers one to Billy, and Billy takes it, whether he wants it or not. Other times, he punches Billy's arm a little harder than Billy likes, grinning, then wanders off as though some mystery that has been puzzling him has been sorted out. Billy is better at most lessons than Horton. Horton sits next to him during prep and copies whatever Billy writes into his own rough book. He knows that Billy knows and will do nothing. He knows that Billy is scared of him, of what he might do if Billy doesn't let him look. One day, when Billy turned over the page too fast

– not really on purpose, just testing Horton to see what he would do – Horton got his compass out and stuck the point into Billy's leg, deep enough to make it bleed.

Now, though, he's offering Billy half a Crunchie and saying they can be friends if Billy wants. Billy takes the Crunchie, but doesn't know how to answer. He doesn't like the sickly orange sweetness of Crunchies, the way they crumble and go soft in your mouth, the way they hollow out, but he badly wants a friend, so badly even Horton will do. When he nods, finally, and says, 'All right, if you like,' Horton snorts. 'You're barmy, you are,' he says, then saunters off to the next class, leaving Billy standing by himself. He waits by the classroom door, talking to Sharples, looking over his shoulder at Billy. They both begin to laugh. Sharples makes the shape of a gun with his hand and points it straight at Billy's head. '*Poum*,' he says. The melting Crunchie is sticky and soft in Billy's fingers. He'd drop it, kick it under a radiator, but he won't give Horton an excuse to hurt him, won't be seen rejecting the gift. He slides his hand, with the piece of Crunchie hidden inside it, into his blazer pocket. His mother will kill him when she sees what he's done.

The hissing starts after tea that evening, a hissing in his ear that gets worse when he shakes his head. He thinks it's the telly at first – he's watching *Thunderbirds*; it might be one of the rockets. It is inside his ear, like something trapped, almost too quiet to hear at first, more like a tickle than a noise, then louder, so that he can't concentrate on what he's watching. His mother is sponging the lining of his pocket and asking him for the hundredth time what on earth he thought he was doing. He hasn't told her how they bully him. He knows what she'll do if he does. She'll go to the headmaster and make a fuss. Then everyone will know and he'll never be left alone again.

'Are you listening to me?' she says. He nods, then winces as the noise in his head turns into pain. 'Because I really ought to tell your father, you know,' she says. 'We can't buy you a new blazer every time you decide to get melted chocolate all over it. Thank goodness it's on the inside.' She looks across. 'Are you all right?' she says, her voice changed. He's about to nod again, but the pain blocks him. 'No,' he says. 'I've got a headache.' She puts the blazer down, touches his forehead with her damp cool hand. 'I'll get you half an aspirin,' she says. 'That should help.' He has the oddest sensation that if he lifted his own hand to touch hers, to hold the comfort of her hand where it was, he would have to strain to reach it, it would be very far away, as far away as her voice. 'Yes,' he says, and his own voice is as distant as hers, lost behind the hiss. He presses his face into her apron, the way he did when he was small, as close as he can get.

That night he dreams about Mitchell, the Head Boy. They are standing together at the edge of an enormous field, watching a game being played that Billy has never seen before and can't understand the rules of. He knows that he and Mitchell are about to be called onto the pitch. He turns to run away but Mitchell leans down towards him and grips his arm. His hand is strong. He squeezes Billy's arm and Billy understands that this ought to hurt. But it doesn't. Somehow, he knows that Mitchell won't hurt him. 'I don't want to play this,' he says, 'I hate games,' but now Mitchell looks impatient. 'It isn't up to you,' he says. His tone is kind but weary. He pulls Billy onto the pitch. There is a noise behind them, of people cheering. The pitch becomes narrower, as though someone is rolling it up like a carpet at each side, leaving a central furrow into which all the players are forced, a furrow that leads to a hole going deep into the earth. Mitchell is very close to him; Billy can feel the heat of bare golden skin on his own skin. The teams stop playing to watch them approach. When they reach the centre of the pitch, with barely enough room to move, Mitchell turns and Billy sees that his back is opening up and becoming wings. 'Hold on,' Mitchell says and begins to rise from the earth, the wings beating slowly, immensely heavy and yet there they are, already high above the pitch, high above the hole, and Billy is attached to Mitchell by a string coming out of his chest and entering the other boy's, at the level of the heart. If it breaks, he thinks, I'll fall and die.

The first time he stole a magazine he did it on impulse. Nobody was looking and he was afraid they might not let him buy it. It looked too old for him. He would be eleven in two months' time. He glanced round the shop. He'd come in for the new monsters comic and some sweets, but someone had made a mistake and put this other magazine where the one with the monsters ought to be and his hunger had passed when he saw the man on the rocks. The colours on the cover were bright, the writing jagged, thrilling in a way he didn't understand. He couldn't take his eyes off it. Before he knew what he was doing he'd slipped it under his blazer and shifted his satchel across, to hide it. Outside, still shocked by what he'd done, but excited too, as though he'd been given an unexpected gift, he darted round to the back of the shop and slipped the magazine between his school books. On the bus home that evening, when everyone else had got off and he was alone on the back seat, he took it out and started to read the stories inside, but his eye was constantly distracted by pictures like the picture on the cover. He almost missed his stop. Shaking, he slid the stolen magazine back into his satchel. He knew that he would have to hide it from everyone, his parents most of all.

'You owe me,' says Horton, pushing him up against the wall.

'What for?' says Billy.

'For that Crunchie.'

'I don't,' says Billy. 'You gave it to me.'

'I what?' Horton turns round. 'Did you hear that?' he says. Sharples comes over.

'Hear what?'

'He says I gave him a Crunchie.'

'It was half a Crunchie anyway,' says Billy. He's still half dreaming, still floating above the rolled-up pitch, or he wouldn't have answered back. Sharples steps up swiftly, his red face inches from Billy's, and punches him in the stomach.

'I didn't ask you,' he says while Billy struggles for breath. 'You speak when you're spoken to.'

'He owes me,' says Horton.

'How much?'

Horton grins. 'How much has he got?'

Sharples jerks Billy upright, lifts him until only his toes touch the ground. 'You look,' he says. Horton looks disgusted, then pushes his hands into the pockets of Billy's shorts while Billy wriggles. He pulls out a fistful of coins, shows them to Sharples.

'Is that all you've got?' says Sharples.

Billy nods.

'Is that enough to pay you back what he owes you?'

Horton shakes his head.

Sharples drops Billy, then holds him by the throat. 'You'd better have it tomorrow or I'll do you over. Have you got that?'

Billy nods. I hate you, he thinks. I hate you, and I will make you pay. I will make you pay for this.

He gets to school late the next morning, hanging around outside the school gates until he hears the bell, then belting across the yard and squeezing in through the assembly-hall door as someone tries to close it. He stands at the end of the row of his form, staring ahead. Last in, first out, he thinks, but as soon as the assembly is over, Wolf catches him by the collar.

'Not so fast, my lad,' he says. 'I saw you sneak in. What kept you?'

'My dad was late leaving me,' says Billy. 'It's not my fault.'

Wolf raises an eyebrow. 'You'd better tell your dad to come and see me at break then, hadn't you? Unless you'd like to stand in for him? Take your punishment like a man?'

I can tell him, thinks Billy. I can tell Wolf what they're going to do to me. It's his job to protect schoolboys. But he knows he can't. 'Yes, sir,' he says. When Wolf walks off, reaching into his jacket pocket for his cigarettes, Billy's hand flies up to catch him, to hold him back, but then falls away. There is no point.

Outside, they are waiting, not by the assembly-hall door where someone might see them, but down the corridor, outside the changing rooms. The Lees twins, Sharples, Horton, two or three other boys who always hang around with them when they hit someone. Billy hesitates. If they haven't seen him, he can sneak round the back of the art room and work his way through the bins and the piles of broken desks to the front of the school where one of the masters might notice him. If that happens he'll still be in trouble but at least he'll be protected until they've gone off and found someone else to hurt. He should have stayed with Wolf. Everyone is scared of Wolf.

Too late. He's been spotted. 'Come over here, Gobface,' Sharples says. 'We've got something to show you.'

He turns and runs down the corridor, his heart thumping. He knows they'll follow, but where else can he go? And then he remembers the niche. Before they have time to turn the corner, he has slipped behind the store cupboard, next to the radiator, and is hunkered down with his face turned to the back of the cupboard, the heat of the radiator on the nape of his neck, its gentle, insistent hiss in his ear. His eyes are closed to hold in tears. Behind the hiss, he can make out a hurried breathing, which must be his although it seems to be at a distance, some little way away from him, where the wall should be. There seems to be more room than he remembers, as though the niche has relaxed for him, welcomed him somehow. He crouches down, opens his eyes, waits for his heart to calm in the unexpected darkness. You're safe now, he hears himself say, or thinks he does.

Then, all at once, there is silence. He lets his breath out slowly. Safe, he thinks again, and a voice, like the echo of his own, says *safe*. He strains to hear where it came from but all further sound is drowned out by the racket of their shoes on the floorboards beyond the cupboard and Sharples saying he'll kill the little fucker when he finds him. *And I'll kill you*, says the voice, so close to Billy's ear he can feel the words' warmth on his skin, like water almost, something liquid, a soothing touch. A strengthening touch. 'He's here,' says someone – it sounds like one of the Lees twins – and Billy flinches, the voice is so near. They must be standing on the other side of the cupboard. 'I can smell him,' says the voice and one of the other boys giggles. 'Stinky Baby Billy,' says Sharples. 'Baby Billy's done a poo in his pants,' says Horton. There is a grinding, dragging sound, as they pull the cupboard away from the wall. Billy closes his eyes again, straightens up, steps back into where the wall ought to be, but he must have miscalculated. He takes another step, hands reaching round behind him into the unexpected emptiness. Slowly, heart pumping, he opens his eyes to the light that should be flooding in as the heavy cupboard is shifted away from the wall, all four boys tugging and pushing to move it, to reach their prey. But there is darkness, just like before, dark as the hole in the field. I've gone blind, he thinks, and then, stretching his arms back as far as they can go, encountering nothing, I've gone mad. Something in his body knows that where the cupboard stood to protect him there is now only open space and the four boys standing there and staring at a radiator, at a wall, and not seeing Billy. He is there, in front of them, as they are in front of him, but he isn't there as well. He is somewhere else, somewhere safe, somewhere they will never reach unless he wants them to. He strains to see them and gradually, as though a veil has been lifted to be replaced by a finer veil, they are lined up before him, shoulder to shoulder, their faces distorted by bewilderment, anger and disappointment, and what might be fear. For a moment, he sees the face of the prisoner of war, roped to the rock, surrounded by the waving saw-edged claws of the crabs, and the face is no longer that of the man, but Horton, Horton wincing as the crab bites into the soft flesh of his thumb, rips at the flesh with its pincers. I'm free, he thinks, as they step away, push the cupboard back against the wall.

He waits maybe five minutes, maybe longer, then edges out through the gap that's been left, as if for him. The corridor is empty. He will be late for his first lesson, but that doesn't frighten him, although it should. And he'll be seeing Wolf at break, but that doesn't frighten him either. He feels invisible, protected. Walking along the corridor, past the changing rooms, he catches a trace of the scent from that first day at school, when he saw the big boys coming back from rugby, that mix of liniment and sweat, a scent that's almost sweet but with an edge of bitterness to it; a scent that gives him strength.

'And I'll kill you,' Billy says.

*

After school that day, he goes to the shop. He has ten minutes before the bus arrives. The tuck money his father gave him in the morning is still in his pocket. He's passed the day in a sort of haze. No one has spoken to him, or threatened him. Sharples and the others have kept their distance; he doesn't know why, but he imagines they can also sense this haze, this protective cloak, invisible to others as he was invisible to them. There is no one he can talk to about what happened that morning, but that's all right. He doesn't need to talk. Besides, he can still hear the voice he heard in the niche. All he has to do is think the words he wants to say to hear the voice reply to him. He's tried it on and off all day. Small questions, nothing of any importance. Sometimes the voice is evasive, sometimes not. He won't tell Billy his name, for example. Other than that, it's like having a friend.

The shop's almost empty, apart from two girls in convent uniform, who glance at him and then look away. He puts his cap in his pocket, walks across to the rotating stand that holds the magazines and starts to swivel it slowly, one eye on the woman behind the counter. She knows him, she knows his mother, she's greeted him with her usual smile. The monster comics he normally buys are in the bottom racks, the weekly magazines his mother reads – recipes, knitting patterns – are at chest height, but he looks above them, moving the rack clockwise, until he sees the new issue of *Rugged Men*. He edges round until the stand is blocking the woman's view of him, lifts the issue carefully from the rack and slides it beneath his open blazer, buttons it, then moves his satchel round until it is hanging in front of him, like a shield. His arm pressed close into his side, he walks towards the door. He's almost reached it when the woman looks up. 'Not found what you're looking for, dear?' Startled, he shakes his head. 'Well, maybe next time,' she says. 'Say hello to your mother for me, won't you?' He nods.

He's waiting at the bus stop, the unopened magazine safely concealed inside his blazer, when someone grabs his elbows from behind. A knee forces itself into the middle of his back. He cries out in surprise, in the first shock of pain. The two convent girls, coming out of the shop, glance over, then walk away as if they have seen nothing. Help me, he thinks, and the voice says, *All in good time*, as his arms are wrenched so hard he's afraid they'll pop out of their sockets. He's waiting to feel the magazine slide from beneath his blazer, still buttoned up, to hear it hit the floor. He's terrified of what they'll do when they find it between their feet, like proof of what he is. 'We saw what you did, you little thief,' says Horton, but he's speaking from some place over to the left, so he can't be the one who's holding Billy. 'We saw you nick that magazine. Didn't we, Sharpie?'

Suddenly released, Billy stumbles forward and is only held up by the strap of his satchel as Sharples attempts to twist it free of Billy's shoulders. Billy hangs on to it.

'Leave me alone,' he says, his voice high-pitched with anger. He's about to shout but something, some fear of being found out, dissuades him. But the magazine, the proof of what he's done, is nowhere to be seen. All he can see when he looks down is his cap, lying on the pavement by his feet. He'll be in trouble if he's caught without it. He sees the Lees twins on the other side of the road, heavy and dumb like the golems he has read about in his comic, waiting to cross.

'You give that here,' says Sharples, finally tearing the satchel away. Billy flies at him, but Horton has caught the edge of Billy's blazer and holds him back. 'Ooh,' says Sharples, 'Baby Billy's lost his rag.' He taunts Billy, holding the satchel out, whipping it away, waving it in the air just out of Billy's reach as Billy struggles to free himself, afraid that his blazer might rip as Horton clings to the hem of it. He feels the buttons about to give.

'What's going on here?'

The three boys turn.

'Cat got your tongues?' says Mitchell. He takes the satchel off Sharples and returns it to Billy. 'This is yours, isn't it?'

'Yes,' says Billy. The dream-string tugs at his heart. *Yes*, says the voice.

'That looks like your bus.' Mitchell glances behind Billy. 'I'll deal with these two,' he says, then points to the pavement. Billy's heart stops. 'Don't forget your cap.'

Billy picks up his cap, then runs for the bus without turning round. When the bus pulls away he opens his satchel and finds the magazine.

In his room that night, with the lights out and the torch on, Billy looks at the magazine. The cover shows a shirtless man hanging by his wrists in a dungeon. Behind him a woman in Nazi uniform is wielding a bullwhip. 'Blood for the harlots of horror,' says the caption. *Yes*, says the voice. *This is for you.*

Hands trembling a little, the torch held under his chin, he turns to the story on page 64.

They waste no time the next day. Billy is taken behind the dining hall at morning break. The Lees twins hold his arms and Sharples slaps his face a couple of times, then punches his stomach until he's crying, spluttering snot from nose and mouth, his knees jerking up in a vain attempt to protect himself from the blows. When Sharples has finished, Horton spits in Billy's face. The twins let him go, but not before they've been through his pockets and taken the money his father gave him that morning. Winded, he slumps to the ground, gasping for breath, his arms cradling his stomach. Sharples kicks him at the base of his spine. 'And that's for being a fucking cry-baby,' he says, while the other three laugh. Horton drops to his knees beside Billy and rubs the spit round his face with the flat of his hand. He has a plaster on the ball of his thumb, slimy and cold, a different texture from the skin. 'And that's for not saying thank you to Sharpie,' he says, before hawking and spitting again. 'Hello, Gobface.' More laughter. Billy closes his eyes, sniffs back the snot in his nose and throat, waits for them to leave him, because sooner or later this will be over, and he will make them pay for what they have done. He will have his revenge. *Revenge is sweet*, his friend says. He's promised him revenge. Oh yes, he says, too weak and winded to move, in too much pain. *Oh yes.* Curled up on himself, he imagines Sharples, shirtless, swinging from a beam, his shoulders twisted out of joint, his body streaked with weals from the bullwhip, a puddle of fresh blood on the floor. He imagines Horton, naked and shivering in the corner of the room, begging for mercy, knowing his turn will come, and the Lees twins, locked in a cage like dogs, their bodies streaked with dirt. All in good time.

He's struggling to his feet when Matron walks round the corner of the dining hall. 'You shouldn't be here, boy,' she says. When he's vertical, she snaps, 'Stand up straight. Don't slouch.' She takes him by the shoulder, forces his face up with her free hand. 'Dear God, boy,' she says, her voice changed. 'What have they done to you?' He lowers his eyes. 'Come with me. Let's get you cleaned up.' She takes him by the arm and leads him away, across the yard that separates the dining hall from the rest of the school, before a line of boys outside the tuck shop, who turn and stare. One of the Lees twins stands among them, waiting to spend the money he's stolen. Billy sees a nervous, imploring smile cross his face before he turns his eyes away.

In the sickroom, Matron takes his blazer off and begins to sponge dirt off the back of it. 'Wash your hands and face over there,' she says, pointing to a basin. He tucks his tie between two shirt buttons, winces as the end of it touches his bare stomach. 'Wait a minute,' she says, and unbuttons his shirt, while he stands there, letting her handle him, no will to resist. He's barely there. He's been reduced to pain and the friend in his head, who is telling him to be patient and to say nothing. *All in good time.* When she shakes her head and asks him who on God's earth is responsible for this, he stares at her as though she is speaking some language that intrigues him and that might be essential for his well-being but that makes no sense. He can feel what might be the start of a smile as she buttons his shirt back up and leads him across to the stretcher at the side of the room. 'Lie down here,' she says, her voice almost gentle but distant, as if she doesn't want to be there either. 'I'll be back in a minute.'

He spends the next two days in his own bed. He refuses to name his bullies and he isn't sure if he's being kept at home because he's covered in bruises or as punishment. His mother has told him how brave he is, which isn't true, and that he is her little hero, and that everything will be all right in the end, which made him cry as soon as he was alone, because he knew that it wasn't true unless he did something to make it true. His father has said that he'll sue the school for negligence, which scared Billy, and that Billy should have stood up for himself, which hurt him, but neither of them has suggested he leave, and he's glad of that. He wants to get back to school as soon as he can because he's been working on ways of getting his revenge. *Rugged Men* has helped. Alone in his room, he takes his new copy out and thumbs through it until he finds the stories he wants, the ones with pictures of men being hurt. He reads what is done to them by Nazis, Japanese guards, prison officers – most of their persecutors are half-naked women, but he imagines himself in their place. Billy holding the whip, Billy releasing the starved rats into the cage, Billy tightening the rope around the thighs. He puts the terrified faces of his tormentors onto the straining, sweat-shiny bodies of the victims. He listens to them as they cry out for mercy, relishing each desperate plea. He imagines Mitchell by his side, golden, immense, scented with liniment, handing him pincers to tear out their nails, and teeth. He talks to his friend, his friend nods yes, encourages him to go on. *They deserve it.* There is an industrial meat-grinder in the corner of the dungeon, large enough to take the body of a grown man. There is a pit in the centre of the floor, and no one knows what it might contain, not even Billy, although he's working on it. Its time will come.

He's telling his friend what he will do to Lees One when his mother comes into the bedroom. 'There's someone here to see you,' she says.

'Who?' He's startled. There is no one he wants to see.

'A friend from school.'

She turns round and smiles behind her, then steps aside to let Horton in. He is wearing jeans and a sweater; Billy almost doesn't recognise him.

'Hello, Billy,' he says.

Billy doesn't know Horton's name. He nods, then looks at his mother, pleading for her not to leave.

'Would you like some orange squash?' she says. 'A slice of cake?'

'Thank you, Mrs Lender.' Horton walks over to the bed. Billy struggles into a sitting position, pulling his pyjama jacket around him.

'What day is it?' he says.

Horton sits on the edge of the bed. 'It's Saturday, you spastic. Otherwise I'd still be at school.' He glances across at the door. Billy can hear his mother downstairs, closing the fridge door. 'You kept your mouth shut then,' he says. 'That's good. People hate kids that tell tales.'

'They sent you, didn't they?'

Horton shakes his head, pulls a dismissive face. 'They'd think I was mad if they knew I'd come to your house like this. They're shitting themselves, to be honest. You should see them. They think you're bound to have grassed them up.' He grins. 'I *am* mad. For all I know you might have talked to your dad, told him what they've done. He's downstairs, watching the wrestling. Like my dad does. It's just like being at home.'

'You did it too.'

Horton looks surprised. 'I never touched you.'

'Yes, you did. You spat in my face.'

'Yes, well, that's like sticks and stones, isn't it? I mean, spit's like words, it doesn't hurt, does it?' He's still grinning. He looks down, picks at the plaster on his thumb.

'You've hurt yourself,' says Billy.

'It's nothing,' says Horton. 'I don't even know how I did it. Do you want to see?'

Billy shakes his head, but Horton has already peeled away the plaster to show a jagged cut, almost an inch long, as though a gobbet of flesh has been torn away.

'Pretty, isn't it?' Horton says. He puts the plaster back over the wound, then reaches across to Billy. Billy flinches. 'I only want to see what they did to you,' he says. He pulls the jacket open, sees the bruises that Sharples' fists have left on the skin. 'Crikey,' he says. 'I bet that hurt.'

'What do you want?'

Billy's mother comes back into the room, carrying a tray.

'Here you are, boys,' she says. 'It's cherry cake; I made it this morning. It's still warm.'

'It looks delicious,' says Horton, standing up to take the tray from her.

'Isn't he a gentleman?' says Billy's mother. 'You're lucky to have such a polite friend, Billy.'

Billy doesn't answer. Horton winks at him, puts the tray down beside the bed. 'Thank you, Mrs Lender.'

Billy is confused. Part of him would like to see Horton as a friend, despite what he's done: the spit, the Crunchie, the betrayal. But another part of him, the stronger part, hates Horton and would like to see him dead. To not see Horton at all, he watches his mother leave the room. When she's gone, Horton sits down on the bed again.

'You're good at nicking stuff,' he says. 'If I hadn't been watching you, I'd never have seen you take that magazine.' He takes a bite of cake. 'This is great,' he says. 'I bet you could steal practically anything, couldn't you?'

Billy shakes his head.

'I bet you could,' says Horton again.

'Why?'

Horton leans in. Billy can see a crumb of cake caught on his upper lip, where Horton has the first fine hairs of a moustache, but resists the urge to brush it off.

'Sharpie's waiting for you,' he says. 'He'll really make you cry next time.'

Billy shrugs. Horton pulls away.

'Unless,' he says.

'Unless what?'

Horton grins, takes another bite from his slice of cake.

'Your mum's a brilliant cook. You should bring some of this to school. For all of us.' He pauses. 'On Monday.'

'I'm not coming to school on Monday,' says Billy. 'Not if I don't want to.' He wants to keep them guessing. He needs to be able to surprise them. He's been talking to his friend. *It's better if they don't expect you*, his friend said, and Billy agrees.

'I bet you could nick some cigarettes,' says Horton.

'I don't smoke,' says Billy.

Now Horton shrugs. What you do doesn't matter, his face says.

'Why should I steal stuff for you?' says Billy.

'Because Sharples will rip your throat out if you don't,' says Horton. He puts his own hand on Billy's throat and squeezes gently. Billy doesn't move. Horton lets him go. 'That's why.'

Billy closes his eyes and sees Sharples falling to his knees, his neck torn open, his eyes turned up to Mitchell, whose arms are red with blood. He nods for him to step away and Mitchell does, his head bowed down. More blood is pumping from Sharples' neck, buckets of it, and Billy is waiting for the flow to stop. When it does and Mitchell is watching him, his hands behind his back, he pushes Sharples' body with his foot, as Sharples did with him, because there has to be balance, it is only fair. It must all be fair, everything must always be fair, he knows that, Mitchell knows that, and his only friend, whose name he still doesn't know but will discover one day soon, will remind him in case he forgets.

When he opens his eyes again, the bedroom is empty, as though Horton had never been there. All that is left is a half-empty glass of orange squash and a few crumbs on a plate.

3

He's left alone for almost a week. Horton sidles up to him
on the first morning back and asks him if he's brought any of
his mum's fantastic fruitcake, but he seems to be joking and
when Billy says no he wanders off. And that's all. He notices
Sharples glance his way more than once, and the Lees twins
jostle him to one side of the corridor as they leave assembly,
but no one speaks to him. Even the other boys seem to be
avoiding him. He's relieved and hurt, as though the only
friends he has are the ones that give him pain. Outside the
classroom, between lessons, at break, in the queue for the
dining hall, he finds himself constantly on the lookout for
Mitchell but, when he sees him, looks sharply away.

When he gets the chance, maybe once every other day, he
hangs around the store cupboard beside the niche. Sometimes,
alone, he shifts it slightly from the wall to make sure there's
still room for him behind it. Yes, it's just as he left it the last
time, when the cupboard was moved away by Sharples and
the others and he stood there staring straight at them and
they couldn't see him. Although that can't have happened.

Nobody can be invisible. He must have dreamt it, he tells himself, but he isn't convinced. He half expects the voice of his friend to tell him off for lacking faith.

This morning, Thursday, he moves the cupboard away from the wall, makes enough room to see in, and then some more, room enough to wriggle into the niche entirely and disappear. The radiator hisses its welcome. He smiles a welcome in return, a sense of relief flooding over him as he slides a first leg through the gap.

'What are you doing?'

Mitchell is standing behind him. Billy starts back but it's too late. Mitchell has caught him halfway into the niche.

'You shouldn't be squeezing yourself into that,' Mitchell says. 'You might get stuck.' He sounds amused. Humiliated, Billy edges out.

'Wait a minute,' says Mitchell. 'I know you.'

Billy looks up into Mitchell's eyes.

'You're the one they were bullying outside the shop, aren't you?'

'Yes, Mitchell.'

'So you know who I am then?'

Billy feels himself blush. 'Yes, Mitchell.'

'You're a new boy, right? First year?'

Billy nods.

'You poor little bugger,' says Mitchell. 'And then they did you over again the next day, didn't they?' He winces in sympathy. 'Properly this time. You're the one, aren't you?'

Billy nods again.

'What's your name?'

'Lender, Mitchell.'

'So is that why you're trying to hide? Afraid they'll get you again?'

'I'm not trying to hide.'

Mitchell laughs. 'Of course you aren't. Well, you can't hide in there, Lender. There's no room.' He gives Billy a playful cuff round the ear, then lets his hand drop onto Billy's shoulder.

'So where are you supposed to be?'

'In French.'

Mitchell looks along the empty corridor.

'With Konk, then. Well, he's all right. It could be worse. It could be Millie. Then you'd really be in hot water. *L'eau chaud.*' Billy's bewildered. *Low show*? Show what? Why low? Mitchell grins. 'That's French for hot water. You ought to know that by now.' He glances at his watch. 'You'd better get your skates on, hadn't you? Or you really will be late.' Billy still doesn't move. Mitchell takes hold of him by both shoulders, swivels him gently until they are standing face to face, or almost, with Mitchell's knees slightly bent, although still not enough for their eyes to be on a level. Mitchell is making an effort to reach him, Billy knows that, but he can't look up any longer. The distance between them is still there, or the opposite of distance, something that draws him in and holds him back at the same time. Because Billy's heart is beating so hard he's convinced Mitchell will pick the beat up through his hands, resting so heavily on Billy's shoulders, and will know what Billy is feeling, the heat of him, and will not understand, as Billy does not understand. There is something going on in his head he can make no sense of, a buzzing he can't quite place.

'You'll be in detention if you don't get a move on.'

It seems to Billy that Mitchell's hands are both holding him up, supporting him, and holding him down, so that he won't float away, float up to the ceiling like a released balloon. Please tell him to leave me now, he says to the voice in his head. Tell him to leave me alone. I'm all right. I only wanted to make sure the niche was still here, just in case. You understand that, don't you? But there is no answer. His new friend isn't listening any longer, or doesn't want to answer. No breath but his, and Mitchell's. Not knowing what else to do, he shrugs; the hands on his shoulders are all he knows.

'Do you want to tell me about something?' Mitchell says, in a lower, coaxing voice, almost a whisper, as though he is talking to a frightened animal. He leans closer in. There is the tang, sharp in Billy's nostrils, of liniment and sweat; of Mitchell. 'Maybe I can help.'

Billy shakes his head.

'Have they hit you again?'

'No.'

'Will you tell me if they do? You don't need to tell anyone else. Just me.'

Billy nods.

'Is that a promise?'

'Yes, Mitchell.'

Mitchell lets his shoulders go. 'You don't need to hide from anyone,' he says. 'Ever. Remember that.'

'I will, Mitchell.' Billy looks up finally, his face breaking into a smile. 'I promise.'

*

51

And then it starts again. Friday afternoon, he's waiting outside the shop for the bus to take him home and there they are, all four of them. This time, Horton takes the lead. He stands close to Billy, so close Billy tries to move away, but his back is already against the wall and the Lees twins have stepped to each side of him. A few feet away, his round face split by a grin, is Sharples. He's carrying his blazer over one shoulder, despite the cold wind. His sleeves are rolled up, his forearms bare and white. He's staring at Billy. Billy drops his eyes. Help me, he says to the friend in his head, but not in his head. The friend in the niche. Tell me what to do.

'We want you to get something for us,' Horton says.

Billy doesn't move, doesn't answer. Horton grabs his balls and squeezes. 'Did you hear me?'

Billy winces, doubles over in pain. 'Yes,' he says, gasping for breath. His voice is higher than normal, squeaky, a girl's voice.

The twins start laughing. 'Baby Gobface,' they say together. The one on the left gets closer, lifts him up straight, turns Billy's face towards his with his free hand and spits. Billy feels the spit on his cheek, feels it soft and warm as it trickles down his skin.

'What do you want me to get?' he says.

Horton steps aside, a little bow from the waist, as Sharples moves in. 'You go into the shop, right.' Billy nods. He wants to wipe his cheek before the spit hits his collar, but doesn't dare. 'You go into the shop,' says Sharples a second time, more slowly, 'and you get four packets of No. 6.'

'I can't do that,' said Billy, trembling. 'All the cigarettes are behind the counter. She'll see me.'

'Don't you worry about that,' says Horton, excited. 'I'll be there as well. I'll keep her busy. You'll just need to be quick.' For a moment, it's as though he and Billy are friends, accomplices, partners in crime. Billy wants to grin at him, ignoring Sharples, ignoring the twins as they fall away, finally giving him room to move. But then Sharples takes him by the arm, gently but firmly, and he's reminded who's the boss. Horton and the twins don't count, Billy thinks; they're like the retainers in the dungeon, the silent ones who hold the whips and branding irons and chains for the ones who really matter. It's down to him and Sharples, he thinks, as he's frogmarched to the shop door.

They're barely inside the shop, Sharples still holding Billy's elbow, when Horton pushes past them both and walks across to the counter. 'Excuse me,' he says. He has what Billy's mum calls a cheeky air about him, hands in his pockets, head cocked to one side, his blond hair ruffled where he's taken off his cap. Billy, reminded of his manners, takes off his, folds it and slips it into his pocket so that both hands are free. The woman behind the counter glances up from her knitting. 'Yes, dear,' she says. 'How can I help?' She doesn't seem to have noticed Billy, who is being led by Sharples towards the further end of the counter, where the cigarettes are stacked. Horton has picked up a bar of chocolate – Billy can't see what kind – and is asking the woman how much it costs. The woman tells him. He moves along the display, picks up another bar, his other hand sliding out of sight. 'What about this one?' he asks. Something in his manner has made her suspicious. She puts her knitting down and leans over to see what he's holding. Sharples pokes Billy in the ribs. 'Now,' he hisses.

Billy edges round behind the counter and reaches up to the shelf where the No. 6 are kept. He can hear Horton's voice to his right, but doesn't dare turn to see what's happening until he is safely back beside Sharples. He tries to push the cigarettes into Sharples' hands, but Sharples pushes them back. 'You keep them until we're outside,' he says. He steps away, walks over to the door, where Horton is waiting for him, and Billy is left, standing alone by the counter, the four packets of cigarettes in his hand. His first thought is to slide them into his pocket, but there is no room for them beside his folded cap. He hides the guilty hand behind his back as the woman turns to look at him, her face concerned, briefly doubtful. 'Are you all right, love?' she says. He nods, too nervous to speak. She looks back towards the door, held open by Sharples, with Horton beside him, neither of them leaving the shop, both of them standing and watching, waiting to see what he will do. 'You aren't with those two, are you?' she says, and he can't tell if she's joking, can't tell what answer might be the one she wants to hear. Behind his back, he can feel the four packets shift in his hand, now slick with sweat, as if they're alive and eager to break free. He smiles uneasily, hoping this will be answer enough. 'You aren't with us, are you?' says Horton, with a grin. Billy is hot, on the point of trembling; he can feel his cheeks flush with blood. He will never forgive them for this. Out of nowhere, the memory of the hole in the field comes back to him, the way he felt when they held him over it and threatened to let him go, the emptiness and the updraught of earth-scented air in his face. All the holes join up, he thinks; somewhere deep below him, all the holes are one.

'Are you hiding something behind your back?' the woman says. Billy shakes his head, but she's walking behind the counter towards him. He can feel the cigarettes slip from his hand as she approaches the edge of the counter. Desperate, he glances across at the door but Sharples and Horton have left the shop and are standing side by side in the street outside, staring in, Horton still grinning, Sharples with a dark, determined look on his face, because Billy has fucked up, because Billy is pathetic, because Billy is letting the four packets of cigarettes fall to the floor as the woman rounds the corner of the counter and grabs his shoulder. 'You little thief!' she says. 'You wicked little thief!'

His father comes to pick him up. He's half expecting to be slapped, or at least shouted at, but all his father does is tell him to get in the car. 'We're going home,' he says. Billy sits there, in the warmth and darkness of the car as it winds along the usual roads and sees nothing, hears nothing but the voice. Because the voice won't shut up, however hard he tries to silence it, to block it out. When his father asks him if the cigarettes were for him or for someone else he starts to cry, and can't speak for the tears in his throat, for the noise in his head. Finally, he says, 'I'm sorry, Dad,' shouting as he tries to make himself heard above the voice, which is telling him to keep quiet, to *not say a word*. His father reaches over to give his leg a comforting squeeze. 'Don't worry, lad,' he says.

'Calm down, you're all right now. Let's get you home, shall we?' But Billy isn't all right, because he knows what he has to do, because the voice keeps telling him; *Bring them to me*, the voice keeps saying, but he doesn't know how to do it. And the voice won't let him go until he does.

On Monday morning at school, through all four classes and break, and then during dinner, with Matron watching him out of the corner of her eye the way she always does, it's just like nothing has happened. No one notices him, no one talks to him. Even the teachers ignore him. He wonders sometimes if he's really there. He remembers that time in the niche when they stared at him without seeing him, when he was there and not there. Is this what it's like? he wonders. Is this what I'll have to do to be safe? Not be here? And so he stays silent, carrying his satchel from class to class, not looking at anyone, trying not to flinch if he hears Sharples shout at someone, or Horton's high-pitched laughter, trying not to see them if they move within his range. At morning break, when the other boys are in the playground, he hovers at the end of the corridor near the niche, just in case, one hand on the back edge of the cupboard, but no one comes near, or no one that matters.

Nothing happens until the first lesson of the afternoon, when the boy sitting next to Billy in History nudges him, then passes him a note. He looks down at the folded piece of paper, torn out of a rough book, but doesn't open it until the end of the lesson. It says,

Cry-baby Butterfingers!!! You did it on purpose!!! Your in the shit!!! We will get you!!! You are DEAD!!! YOU ARE DEAD!!!

It's written in green felt-tip, in quivery letters, as though someone has used the wrong hand to disguise himself. It might be Horton; he can't use his right hand since the ball of his thumb turned septic. Whoever it was, he needn't have bothered. They might just as well have signed it, Sharples or Lees or Horton, because Billy isn't about to show anyone. That would mean explaining. He folds the piece of paper the way it was, and then again, and then again until it won't fold any smaller. He holds it in his hand, like something live that he has caught, a fly perhaps, and can't release, but doesn't know what to do with. He can almost feel it move, under the tips of his fingers, as he hesitates by his desk, too scared to leave the room and go to the next class, too scared to stay and be noticed. He's still there when the next class comes in through the door. It's a sixth-form group, no more than five or six, and Mitchell is with them. He frowns when he notices Billy.

'You shouldn't be in this room,' he says. He walks across and gathers up Billy's books. 'We've got a lesson in here now.' He holds the books out to Billy, who stares at them, stunned for a moment as though they are new to him, before taking them and putting them into his satchel. 'Come on,' says Mitchell, 'run along.'

And Billy runs along. He doesn't stop until he's in the next

57

class. It's only when he puts his books down on the desk that he realises he no longer has the folded note. Hurriedly, he searches his satchel. Nothing. He must have dropped it when he took the books from Mitchell. It will be on the floor, he thinks; it will have been kicked beneath the desk. He's folded it so small no one will see it, and if they do no one will ever know it's his. *Don't worry*, says the voice. *Just bring them to me.*

After school, he hurries to the next stop along the route and catches the bus there, so that no one will see him. He gets home safely. His mother is still annoyed with him about the cigarettes. 'How can I look that woman in the eye?' she says, and 'You're almost eleven; you're old enough to know right from wrong.' He doesn't answer. She lets him watch television, although the evening before she'd threatened to send him to his room as soon as he'd eaten his tea. When his father gets home, they sit on the sofa in front of the fire and watch a film together, an American film that makes them laugh. I would like it to be always like this, thinks Billy, the three of us, safe at home. Before he goes up to bed, his father tousles his hair and his mother hugs him when he gives her his usual goodnight kiss, then fetches him a glass of milk and a slice of cake to take up to bed with him. So he knows he's been forgiven.

That night, in bed, Billy's almost asleep when the hissing starts, so unexpectedly he jerks up in fright. The room is pitch black. He throws back the covers and gets out of bed. His feet are cold on the wooden floor of his bedroom. *That's right,* the voice says. *It's time to act*. He walks towards the wardrobe, feeling his way, following the hiss. He is there and not there, Billy and not Billy; he can't tell any longer if the voice is someone else's or his. All he knows is that he must do what it says. He shifts the wardrobe away from the bedroom wall, as quietly as he can because his parents mustn't be woken up. They will try and stop him, and the voice won't let that happen. No one must know where he is, or where he's going. No one must see him slip through the gap he has made. It is smaller than it should be, and lower; he needs to get down on his knees in the darkness, the bare wood cold through his pyjama bottoms, crawling almost to get where he has to get. And then he is there, with the gently hissing radiator to his right telling him that this is where he should be. In the niche.

Billy turns his face to the rough untreated wood of the cupboard's back, to make sure no one has followed him, no one has heard him, then takes a first blind backward step into the space behind him. He is alone, although he doesn't feel alone. He feels that someone is there, someone good, protecting him. The hissing of the radiator that brought him here has been replaced by the regular sound of breathing, either that other someone or himself, he isn't sure. Holding his own breath, he takes a second step, and then a third, expecting the rear wall of the niche to be there, obstructing him, blocking his way, but not finding it. This can't be real, he thinks, reaching behind himself, hesitant to start with and then more daring, touching nothing. Turning round slowly on his heels, he pushes ahead into an ever-deeper darkness. The breathing he heard before is louder now, surrounds him, drowns out his thoughts. Ever more cautious, he continues to feel his way. He closes and opens his eyes, to make sure the darkness is outside himself, that he hasn't been struck blind. He knows he should be scared, but he doesn't feel scared at all. Something tells him he won't stumble. Without knowing why, after walking for what might be minutes into this space that ought to be a wall but isn't, that is open and soft around him in the darkness, felt-like, padded, he comes to a halt. That's when he feels the hands upon him, touching his cheeks, two cool smooth hands, one on each side, holding his head in a cradle of absolute comfort. *Shall I kill them for you?* says the voice of his only friend, so soft and pure it calms the beating of his heart.

He nods and the hands fall away.

Bring them to me, says the voice.

'How can I do that?'

You will find a way.

Billy opens his eyes to see the room he knows already from the pages of his magazine, the same vaulted ceiling and grey stone walls with rings attached to it at waist level and higher, as high as a man can reach. The hands have left his face, but he isn't alone. Mitchell is leaning against the opposite wall, in rugby kit and a leather apron, his bare arms crossed on his chest. He smiles at Billy, as if to say, you took your time. The open pit is in the centre of the room and above it, attached by a chain to the roof, is a circular cage the size of a boy obliged to crouch. He knows this because Sharples is already in the cage. When he sees Billy he starts to whimper. Billy nods at Mitchell, who turns and takes hold of a wheel attached to the wall beside him. He looks a second time at Billy. Sharples is wriggling, trying to move in the cage, to free himself perhaps, hopeless though that is, but there is no room for movement, not any more. The room is filled with a pungent scent as Sharples shits himself. Billy nods a second time and Mitchell begins to turn the wheel. The noise they hear is less a rattle than a churning, of metal buried deep beneath the earth, of rough chains woken into life after decades, after centuries, of lethargy, waiting for their moment. It drowns out the tinny thread of Sharples' pleading as the cage disappears inside the pit.

Horton comes up to him first thing, before assembly. 'I bet you caught it,' he says. 'I saw your dad come to get you.'

'Leave me alone,' says Billy, looking around for the other three.

'Ooh, "leave me alone",' says Horton in his squeaky voice. 'You really made a mess of it in the shop, you know that. I don't think Sharpie's going to let you get away with it.' He takes hold of Billy's tie, pushes the knot up until Billy can hardly breathe. 'Did you get his little note?'

'You wrote that,' says Billy. 'I know you did.'

Horton shrugs. 'You can't prove it.'

Wolf grabs them both by the hair, tugs until Horton squeals. 'Get into hall, you two,' he says. 'Hanging around here, gossiping like a pair of fishwives.'

During the first hour, Billy sees that Sharples isn't there. His desk is by the window; he keeps glancing out, not concentrating on the lesson, expecting him to come in late, with some excuse, and be given detention. But he doesn't appear. Between lessons, before the second hour starts, he notices the Lees twins standing together in the corridor, clustered with Horton and three other boys. When he approaches, because there is no other way, they stop talking to stare at him, but he walks past, suddenly not caring. Without Sharples, he realises, they're nothing, nobody. Without their master, the Lees twins are mindless, will-less golems. Not even Horton frightens him any longer. In his mind, Billy's still in the room with the cage and the pit, with Mitchell, brave and bold, in his leather apron and the whispering voice of his friend, telling him that everything will be fine. That he only has to be patient.

The next day, at assembly, the headmaster tells them to wait in their classrooms at morning break. As they file out, a boy in the third year whispers that he's seen a police car parked outside and the news runs along the corridor like a trail of fire. There is still no sign of Sharples. Horton comes over to him as they go to the first lesson. 'Hello,' he says, his air suspicious, as though Billy might know something he doesn't. Billy turns away as though he hasn't heard.

At break they go back to their own class, sit there until Wolf arrives. He stalks into the room, his gown billowing behind him. 'I expect you're wondering why you're here,' he says. 'Well, to be honest, so am I. It appears that one of your number has decided to abscond. You may have noticed that young Master Sharples hasn't honoured us with his presence these past two days. I don't suppose any of you wretched children have seen him?' He pauses, sighs. 'I thought not.' He walks across to Horton. 'You're one of his little cronies, aren't you?' he says. Horton nods. 'The police will be talking to you in a few moments, so you'd better put your thinking cap on.' Wearily, he looks round the room. 'Any other *special* friends of Sharples here?' When no one answers, he tells Horton to stand up. 'Well?' he says. 'Perhaps you can help me?' Horton points at the twins, and then, with a smirk, at Billy.

'I'm not his friend,' says Billy. He's about to say more when the voice whispers *Hush*.

The door opens and Mitchell walks in. 'I've come from the police,' he says. Wolf summons Horton, the Lees twins and Billy to the front of the class.

'These are for you,' he says. 'Do with them as you will.' He turns to the rest of the class as Mitchell leads the four boys from the room. 'I shall now explain to the rest of you how many dangers lurk in the outside world,' he begins, 'and what can be done to avoid them.'

Mitchell leads them to a small room beside the headmaster's study. When they pass the cupboard in the corridor, Billy feels a draught of air, warm air, that disappears almost immediately. He glances at the others, but no one else seems to have noticed. The Lees twins look scared. Horton is his usual cocky self. Why did you say we were friends? Billy wants to ask him, but not in front of Mitchell. Having Mitchell there gives him strength.

The four boys are taken into the room together and lined up in front of a table. Behind the table, a policewoman is playing with the cap of a pen. A policeman is leaning against the wall, cleaning his nails with a small file. They smile. 'So you're David's friends?' the policewoman says. For a moment, Billy wonders who she means. The other three nod silently, looking at each other. 'I hope you'll be able to help us,' she continues. 'His mum and dad are very worried.' She pauses. 'We'll need to talk to you one by one but before we do, maybe you can tell us if anything was worrying David?' At this, at the notion that Sharples might *worry*, Billy fights back an urge to laugh. 'No,' says Horton, his voice serious, and the Lees twins shake their heads. 'OK,' she says, then looks directly at Horton. 'We'll start with you, shall we?' Mitchell leads the other three out of the room. 'You wait here,' he says, pointing to a row of chairs. And they do.

Billy is the last to enter. He's been told by the voice what to say. Nothing. It only takes a minute and he's out again. 'That was quick,' says Mitchell, as he takes them back to their classroom. In a lower voice, he adds, 'I didn't expect to see you there. You aren't friends at all, are you?" Billy looks up and smiles.

'No,' he says. 'I hated him.'

The following afternoon is cross-country. Billy's still in the first stretch of the lane, lagging behind with the slow boys from the rest of the school, the smokers and the fatties, when Mitchell and two other prefects appear from the next field along the run and tell them to stop where they are. Nobody asks why. Ten minutes later, the sports master rides up on a bicycle and orders them all back to the school. Some of the faster boys come running back through the gate into the field, but stop when they see the stragglers. One of them waves his arms and shouts out, 'They've found him,' but, when stopped and questioned, doesn't know where. Another boy says he was swinging from a tree, but Billy knows this can't be true. Sharples would never do a thing like that.

They're ordered into the assembly hall and told to stay with the rest of the boys in their year, but not even Wolf can stop them rushing to the windows when they hear cars driving across the playground and the siren of an ambulance. 'They're police cars,' cries the first boy to arrive, clambering onto a pile of chairs to see better. It's only when the headmaster gets onto the stage and shouts for order that the school settles down. Everyone shuffles to his place, except for Billy, who has edged his way to the door and, before anyone can stop him, or try to stop him, if anyone should care, he is running along the corridor towards the playground. He pauses for a second beside the niche, the time it takes to say, Thank you, then skirts the row of wooden buildings that house the lower-form classrooms until he has reached the path leading down to the start of the cross-country route, a strip of land between the rugby pitches and the edges of the school grounds. In the lane outside the grounds, he can see a police car parked, so he stays on his side of the hedge, keeping his head low. He'd get down into the ditch but it's thick with mud and rotting leaves. It rained all yesterday evening and through the night. He must have got soaked to the skin, thinks Billy, smiling to himself as he wriggles between shoulder-high clumps of cow parsley and straggling brambles. He's out of breath by now, stumbling a little as he runs, but he can't remember the last time he felt this happy. He doesn't even mind the dirty water that splashes up his leg as his foot hits an unexpected puddle. He's never done the cross-country route this fast; it's lucky they weren't made to change out of their running kit before being sent into the hall. He wonders if anyone did see him leave, if anyone cared. Mitchell, perhaps. He feels as though Mitchell's eyes are always on him, even if they're in different rooms. He picks up the scent of him in the air, on his clothes, the scent of fresh sweat and liniment, the space he fills in Billy, like a second heart.

It takes him no time at all to reach the ambulance and the other two police cars. Before anyone can spot him, he crouches behind the hedge on his side of the lane. He can see the gate that leads into the field opposite, where the hole in the ground is. He isn't surprised to find them here. He knew this is where they'd all end up. He knew that all the holes would connect. Beyond the gate, men are shouting, but he can't hear what they're saying. All he can hear is a rising tone of alarm. Then two men climb down from the back of the ambulance with a rolled-up stretcher and carry it through the open gate. Half an hour later, maybe more, he watches them carry the stretcher back with the broken body of Sharples draped across it, stark naked and streaked with shit and mud and slime, like something that's just been born.

No one is waiting for Billy when he gets back. He walks into an empty school. He looks in his classroom and thinks about taking his satchel, but decides to leave it where it is. He pops his head into other rooms. Some doors are open, as if the class has just this minute left. Others are closed. The science labs are locked; he wonders why. The assembly hall is deserted, the chairs lined up and ready for the following day. In the gym, the equipment – the horses and trampolines and mats – has been stacked in its usual place at the far end, beneath the high windows you can only see through if you climb a rope almost to the top. The changing room is silent, tidy, everything put away. Even the air smells of nothing. In the showers, the steam has entirely dispersed. Billy wants to call out, to see if anyone will answer, but is scared that no one might. He's about to cross the drive and walk out of the school, to walk towards the bus stop, go home, still in his running kit because he no longer knows where his proper clothes are, his itchy shorts and blazer, his shirt and tie, although surely someone must have found them, and wondered who they belonged to, and thought of looking for him. Perhaps, if he leaves the school now, he might never be found. This is when he hears the voice. *You can't leave now*, it tells him. *We haven't finished yet.* Oh yes I have, he wants to say, I *have* finished, but to whom? I didn't mean it to happen like this, he wants to say, although perhaps he did. But he knows that isn't what the voice wants to hear, because the voice doesn't listen to reason, or excuses or apology, and it is the voice that counts.

And then he hears a hissing noise and understands. There is only one place left that he can go to. He pauses for a final second by the door leading out to the drive, where he first saw Mitchell with the sunlight on his skin, the drive beyond which the road is visible, but it might be a hundred miles away for Billy, as he walks along the corridor and places both hands on the edge of the store cupboard to pull it away from the wall. As he squeezes into the space he has made, to stand beside the radiator, its hissing gets louder, higher pitched, but also less fixed, rising and falling, regular as the ratchets of a turning wheel. Not only the hissing; the heat it throws out is no longer constant, but an even, uninterrupted pulse. The radiator seems to be beating in time with Billy's heart.

He watches the wall dissolve and steps into the darkness.

Some time later, he doesn't know how much, he's woken by the sound of people speaking. He can't tell how far away they are. He's sitting in the room with the vaulted ceiling and the grey stone walls but this time he's alone. He gets up and crosses to the pit in the centre of the room, beneath the empty cage, to see if that's where the noise is coming from, and some of it *does* seem to be coming from there, far down, a low insistent murmuring that might be children, or not even human. But then, above the endless pulse of the hiss, which has never ceased, which was with him while he slept, he hears other voices, voices he recognises, coming from where he came from, from where the wall dissolved. He hears Matron, and Wolf, and Mitchell. To start with, the words aren't clear, but when he hears the word *Lender* he understands. They are talking about him. He's about to run towards them, but some force holds him back, as though he were in the cage himself. The murmuring from the pit is getting louder, drowning out their words. He strains to hear. Then he catches Matron saying 'He must be somewhere' and Wolf is saying something about 'Two in one day' and he wants to tell them he's safe, he isn't like Sharples, but the voice of his friend tells him to hush. *Don't think you're so special*, the voice says in a tone it's never used with Billy before, as though they aren't friends at all. Billy's skin is suddenly cold, his bare legs covered in goosebumps.

He edges away from the murmuring of the pit, less human than ever, a murmuring that has begun to sound like rodents feeding or *the noise of the pit itself*, to get back to where he came from, to reach his niche, his one safe place. He feels his way blindly through the darkness, his hands stretched out before him, ignoring the voice of his friend, ignoring the pit and what might come out of it.

He's almost there when he hears the store cupboard being dragged away from the wall. 'I caught him trying to hide behind here a few days ago', says Mitchell, 'after he'd been bullied,' and Billy's heart leaps. He tries to shout out, Yes, I'm here, but no sound comes. He can't make himself heard above the hissing from the radiator. It can't be far now, he thinks. He's breathing hard. 'I'll look,' says Mitchell.

And then, as if from nowhere, the niche is filled with light and everything it holds – the wall, the floor, the air itself – turns white hot as Mitchell reaches both arms out towards him. 'Come here,' he says, reaching out to take him in, to make him safe, all gold, a niche of gold, and the radiator explodes.

Charles Lambert is the author of several novels, short stories, and the memoir *With a Zero at its Heart*, which was voted one of *The Guardian* readers' Ten Best Books of the Year in 2014.

In 2007, he won an O. Henry Award for his short story 'The Scent of Cinnamon'. His first novel, *Little Monsters*, was longlisted for the 2010 International IMPAC Dublin Literary Award. Born in England, Charles Lambert has lived in central Italy since 1980.